BOYZ RULE!

Basketball Buddies

Felice Arena and Phil Kettle

illustrated by
Gus Gordon

First published 2003 by
MACMILLAN EDUCATION AUSTRALIA PTY LTD
627 Chapel Street, South Yarra, Australia 3141

This edition first published in the United States of America
in 2004 by MONDO Publishing.

For information contact:
MONDO Publishing
980 Avenue of the Americas
New York, NY 10018

Visit our web site at http://www.mondopub.com

07 08 09   8 7 6 5 4

ISBN 1-59336-369-9 (PB)

Library of Congress Cataloging-in-Publication Data

Arena, Felice, 1968-
   Basketball buddies / Felice Arena and Phil Kettle ; illustrated by Gus Gordon.
   p. cm. -- (Boyz rule!)
   Summary: Luis and Billy get together to play basketball, but become involved
   in more than just the game. Includes miscellaneous information related to
   basketball, as well as questions to test the reader's comprehension.
   ISBN 1-59336-369-9 (pb.)
   [1. Basketball--Fiction. 2. Interpersonal relations--Fiction.] I. Kettle, Phil, 1955-
   II. Gordon, Gus, ill. III. Title.
PZ7.A6825Bas 2004
[E]--dc22
                                                                    2004045806

Project Management by Limelight Press Pty Ltd
Cover and text design by Lore Foye
Illustrations by Gus Gordon

Printed in Hong Kong

Contents

Billy   Luis

CHAPTER 1

Wanna Play?

Billy wanders down to his local basketball courts hoping to meet up with his best friend, Luis. Billy wants to shoot a few hoops with him. When Billy arrives, he finds Luis wearing a T-shirt with the name "Michael Jordan" written on the front of it.

Billy "What's up, Luis?"

Luis tosses his basketball at the hoop. It swishes through the net. Billy gestures to Luis to pass him the ball. Luis does. Billy bounces the ball a couple of times then shoots from the foul line. He misses. Luis rebounds and completes the shot. He dribbles the ball in and out between his legs, pretending he doesn't hear Billy asking for the ball. Finally he answers.

Luis "Are you talking to me? My name's Michael Jordan, not Luis. If you wanna play with me, ya have to call me Michael."

Billy (scoffs) "Yeah, right!"

Luis suddenly stops dribbling the ball and walks over closer to Billy.

Luis "Yeah. 'Cause that's who I am."

Billy "Whatever. Aww, your breath stinks, dude. You really need to floss."

Luis glares at Billy and rolls his eyes. He looks annoyed.

Billy "Hey, relax, will ya? I didn't mean to make you mad. I just wanna play basketball."

Luis "Okay, let's go. You against me, one-on-one—first one up to 11. Only half court—back to the center line after you score. And I'm gonna whip your butt, because I'm Michael Jordan!"

Billy "Yeah, whatever. Bring it on."

Luis "I'll even let you start with
the ball. You need all the help you
can get."

CHAPTER 2

Bring It On!

Luis shoves the ball at Billy. Billy begins to bounce the ball by his side. He moves a few paces forward, working out the best way to get past Michael Jordan. Billy suddenly charges toward him, takes a giant lay-up, shoots, and gets a basket.

Billy "Yeah! Two points!"

Luis "Maybe you should buy a lottery ticket, 'cause that was just a fluke!"

Billy "I don't think so."

Billy returns to the center of the court, then again rushes toward Luis. He stops and takes a long shot from outside the three-point line. He misses. Luis rebounds and makes the shot. He now has possession of the ball.

Luis "You were saying? It's two-two! Look out! No stopping me now!"

Luis successfully passes Billy and sinks another one. A few moments later he misses and Billy completes the shot.

CHAPTER 3

A Stolen Shot

It's a fierce, even competition.
The score is soon tied at eight-eight.
Luis has the ball. He signals for a
time-out.

Billy "What's wrong? Why a
time-out?"
Luis "Nothing. I just wanna make
this more interesting."
Billy "What? How?"

Luis "I'm gonna give you a free shot.
But you have to take it from outside
the three-point line. If you get it, it
takes you to 11 and you win."

Billy "What makes you think I need
a free shot?"

Luis "Well, if you don't, I'm gonna
be the winner. I'm just being nice,
that's all."

Billy "Nice! Huh! You're full of it. Nope, no way. I don't want a free shot. I want to beat you fair and square. You're just scared that you're gonna lose."

Luis "Whatever. I know I'd take it if someone gave *me* a free try."

Billy thinks long and hard.

Billy "Fine, I'll do it…but to make it less of a freebie, if I miss, then you automatically win."

Luis "Cool, if you want to make it even easier for me. You're on. Take your shot, loser."

Billy "Where's the ball?"

The basketball is nowhere to be seen. The boys look up and see that in the distance another boy, who had snuck up on them while they were talking, has stolen the ball and is now running away with it.

Luis "Come back, you dirty
rotten..."

Luis chases after the thief. Billy
follows.

CHAPTER 4

Showdown

Luis and Billy chase the thief out of the courts and down several streets until they finally catch up to him at the driveway of his house—where he has taken cover and protection behind two older boys.

Billy "Now what are you gonna do?"

Luis "I'm gonna ask for my ball back, that's what!"

Billy "Are you crazy? They don't look like the types to just hand it over."

Luis "Yeah, well...we'll see."

Luis leaves Billy and confidently struts toward the older boys and the younger thief hiding behind them. A few moments later he returns to Billy—without his ball.

Billy "So? What happened? What did they say?"

Luis "You're right. They're not gonna give my ball back, unless…"

Billy "Unless what?"

Luis "They said the only way I can get my ball back is if we play them for it—us against them. In their driveway. See? They've got a hoop and backboard above their garage door. We have to win if I ever want to see my ball again."

Billy "But they're like twice as big as us. They'll murder us."

Luis "Oh, duh! No kidding."

Luis starts to wander back in the direction of the basketball courts.

Billy "Hey! Where are you going?"

Luis "Home."

Billy "What about your ball? You can't just let them have it."

Luis "Why not? They're going to beat us anyway."

Billy "I don't believe this! What happened to Mr. Tough Guy back at the courts? You can't just walk away. You're Michael Jordan! Come back. I've got a plan."

CHAPTER 5

Dangerous Play

Billy tells Luis to move closer to him.

Luis "So, what's your big plan?"
Billy "Follow me and just do what
I say."

Billy walks over toward the older boys, with Luis only a few steps behind him. He tells the boys that he and Luis are willing to take up their challenge and play them for the ball.

Billy "And since we're younger, we think it's only fair that we start off with the ball."

The older boys sneer and chuckle amongst themselves. They agree with Billy's request and toss the basketball to him. Billy gets into position as if he is about to play, and gestures to Luis to do the same. Luis is totally confused. He shoots Billy a look as if to say, "Are we really going to play these guys?" Suddenly, Billy yells at the top of his lungs...

Billy "RUN!!"

Billy charges off down the street
with the ball in his hands. Luis
suddenly realizes what has just
happened and sprints after him. The
older boys look stunned, but soon
give chase.

Billy (panting) "Quick! Run! Run!"

Billy and Luis quickly duck down an alley, scramble over a fence, cross a major highway on a footbridge, then quickly hide behind a large billboard, located by the side of the freeway. Several minutes pass by.

Billy "I think we lost them. Here's your ball."

Luis "You can keep it. I've got another one at home. It was a cool idea you had back there—crazy, but cool. Thanks, Billy."

Billy (smiling) "No problem."

Time ticks by. Billy and Luis feel it's safe to leave their hiding spot.

Billy "Hey, look!"

Both boys look up to see that on the front of the billboard is an advertisement with a photo of the real Michael Jordan on it. They smile and make their way back to the basketball courts.

Billy "So, I still have my free shot."

Luis "Yeah. You still have to lose
our game!"

When the boys reach the basketball
courts, Luis remembers he should
have been home an hour ago.

Luis "Gotta bolt. See ya!"

Billy "Hey! What about our game—
my free shot?"

Luis "Let's call it a draw."

Luis heads off home, leaving Billy staring at the ring.

Billy takes a step behind the three-point line. He aims and shoots. He misses the backboard completely.

Billy (whispering to himself) "Yeah, let's call it a draw."

Luis

BOYZ RULE!
Basketball
Lingo

Billy

assist A pass by one player to another that results in the second player scoring.

backboard The transparent glass or wooden backing to which the basket is attached.

bench Where the reserve players on the team sit.

dribbling The way a player moves the ball down the court by bouncing it up and down.

free throw area The rectangular area under the basket between the free throw line and the end of the court.

traveling When a player runs while holding the ball and not dribbling. Traveling is a penalty.

BOYZ RULE!

Basketball Musts

☞ You should always try to be on the team with the tallest players.

☞ If you get stripped, you don't have your clothes taken off. You have the ball taken from you!

☞ There are usually five players on a team, but you can have as many players as you want in a team of park basketball.

☞ A steal is when the ball is taken away from you during play, not when you decide you like your friend's basketball and take it home. If you do that, you will not be able to play one-on-one anymore and your friend will probably not still be your friend.

☞ Always give a high five when you shoot a basket.

☞ Always try to do slam-dunks.

☞ Remember, when you dribble, it is with the basketball and not with spit down your chin!

☞ If someone yells "foul," it means that you have done something wrong—it doesn't mean that your mother has arrived at the court with a chicken sandwich.

BOYZ RULE!
Basketball
Instant Info

The NBA stands for the National Basketball Association. It was formed in 1946 and came up with many of the rules that are still used in basketball today.

The record for the tallest ever basketball player is 8 feet, 1/2 inch (2.45 meters).

Michael Jordan holds the record for the highest point-per-game average in the NBA—31.5.

The highest winning score in an NBA game is 186.

The most basketballs ever dribbled by the same person at the same time is six.

Basketball got its name because the first hoops were empty peach baskets.

Basketball was invented by James Naismith in 1891. Naismith was a teacher at a boy's school in Massachusetts who wanted a game that could be played in winter, indoors. He came up with basketball.

Women's basketball began in 1892.

Women's basketball was first played in the Olympics in 1976.

Think Tank

1 Which famous basketball player does Luis pretend to be?

2 How do Luis and Billy get their ball back from the older boys?

3 What is a slam-dunk?

4 What do you do when you dribble?

5 How many players are there on the court at one time?

6 What are "time-outs" for?

7 Do you think Luis and Billy should have played against the older boys? What do you think would have happened if they had?

8 Do you think boys or girls are better basketball players? Why?

Answers

1 Luis pretends to be Michael Jordan.

2 They pretend they are going to play and then, when the older boys give them the ball to start the game, Billy yells "RUN," and they run, hide, and get back the ball.

3 A slam-dunk is when you jump up to the hoop and slam the ball through it without shooting it.

4 When you dribble, you bounce the ball on the ground as you move around the court.

5 There are 10 players on the court at any one time—5 from each team.

6 Time-outs are chances for the coach or players to discuss strategies that will help them win. They are also times for pep talks.

7 Answers will vary.

8 Answers will vary.

- If you got most of the answers correct, then you might be ready for the NBA.

- If you got more than half of the answers correct, you should play on your local team.

- If you got less than half of the answers correct, then go down to the park and practice with your best friend.

Felice →   ← Phil

Hi Guys!

We have lots of fun reading and want you to, too. We both believe that being a good reader is really important and so cool. Try out our suggestions to help you have fun as you read.

At school, why don't you use "Basketball Buddies" as a play and you and your friends can be the actors. Set the scene for your play. What props do you need? Maybe a basketball, or just use your imagination to pretend that you are at the stadium and about to play in the NBA.

So...have you decided who is going to be Billy and who is going to be Luis? Now, with your friends, read and act out our story in front of the class.

We have a lot of fun when we go to schools and read our stories. After we finish, the kids all clap really loudly. When you've finished your play your classmates will do the same. Just remember to look out the window—there might be a talent scout from a television station watching you!

Reading at home is really important and a lot of fun as well.

Take our books home and get someone in your family to read them with you. Maybe they can take on a part in the story.

Remember, reading is a whole lot of fun.

So, as the frog in the local pond would say, Read-it!

And remember, Boyz Rule!

Felice

BOYZ RULE!
When We Were Kids

Phil

Felice "Did you ever play one-on-one as a kid?"

Phil "Yes, against the brick wall."

Felice "I bet that wasn't as hard as playing against the Harlem Globe Trotters."

Phil "Did you play one-on-one against the Harlem Globe Trotters?"

Felice "No, but I did go and see one of their shows once. I learned to spin the ball on one finger from watching them. Bet your brick wall couldn't do that!"

Phil "Guess not, but it was the best in the world at blocking."

What a Laugh!

Q Why did the chicken cross the basketball court?

A Because the referee was calling fouls.